THE Legend OF
DIAMOND LIL

A J.J. Tully Mystery

DOREEN CRONIN

illustrated by

KEVIN CORNELL

BALZER + BRAY
An Imprint of HarperCollins *Publishers*

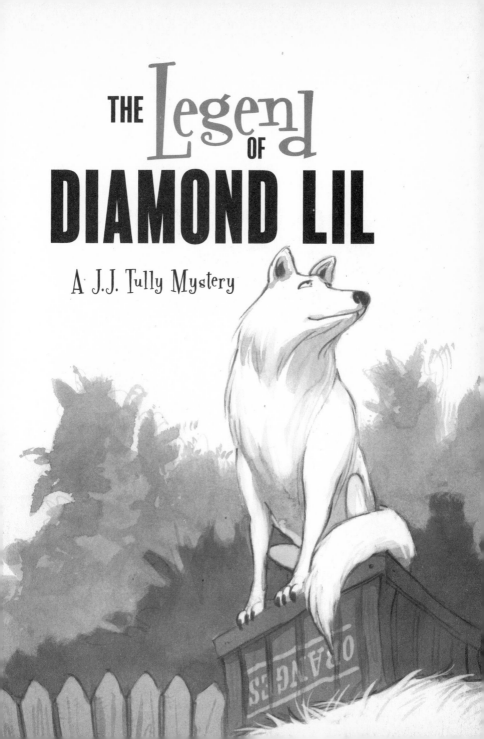

THE Legend OF DIAMOND LIL

A J.J. Tully Mystery

ALSO BY DOREEN CRONIN:

The Trouble with Chickens:
A J.J. Tully Mystery

Balzer + Bray is an imprint of HarperCollins Publishers.

The Legend of Diamond Lil: A J.J. Tully Mystery
Text copyright © 2012 by Doreen Cronin
Illustrations copyright © 2012 by Kevin Cornell

Library of Congress Cataloging-in-Publication Data is available.
ISBN 978-0-06-177996-1 (trade bdg.) — ISBN 978-0-06-198578-2 (lib. bdg.)

Typography by Carla Weise
12 13 14 15 CG/RRDH 10 9 8 7 6 5 4 3 2 1
❖
First Edition

For Christina & Amanda
—D.C.

To Mom and Dad, for their Moosh-like
parenting
—K.C.

CONTENTS

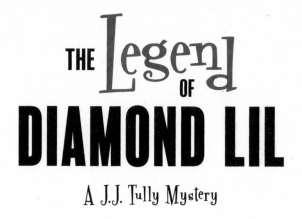

THE Legend OF DIAMOND LIL

A J.J. Tully Mystery

Night Shift

A week ago, I woke up in a quiet country yard that smelled like fresh air and dog pee. It was a place where fluffy young chicks felt safe and a fellow like me could get a good night's sleep—the kind of sleep that a retired search-and-rescue dog ought to have earned by now.

But that was before the possum showed up.

Skunks, possums, rats, and raccoons—the country is full of 'em—and every last one of them will do things to a chicken that no soft-boiled kid should ever see.

She was three feet from the chicken coop. How she got past me in the first place, I couldn't know—at the time.

I was across the yard in less time than it takes for a burp to clear the space between my mouth and my nose. She twisted her body around and showed me her sharp, dangerous smile through a hiss.

In that moment, I knew she was a problem.

She wasn't the first predator to take a chance in my yard.

But she was the only one who had come back a second time.

A couple years back—before I was here to make any kind of difference—Barb had lost a

whole flock of chickens to a possum.

We were out on a search-and-rescue drill and I could tell something was not right.

I heard her tell one of the other handlers what she had found in her yard that morning.

She had been shaken up by that loss. And it wasn't going to happen again.

Not as long as I was here.

I pounced and the possum ran—straight up the fence and out of sight.

If I had followed her, I would have found the real trouble that was lurking next door. Instead, it found me.

The Usual Suspects

I came home from my morning walk to find a chicken blindfolded and tied to a piece of rawhide. Six months ago, I would have found this disturbing. That was before I met Dirt and Sugar, two popcorn-colored chicks who lived with their mom, Moosh, and a matching set of popcorn-colored chicks in the coop across the yard.

There were two plastic cups on the floor.

Neither of the cups smelled like anything I wanted near my food bowl.

"Why?" I grunted.

"Search-and-rescue practice," answered Sugar.

"Why can't you do this at home?" I asked.

"Mom doesn't like the smell," replied Sugar.

"I don't like the way you smell either," I muttered.

"The smell of the *cups*," said Sugar with an eye roll.

I was about to kick them out when something about the blindfold Dirt was wearing caught my eye.

I expected a rag or maybe a sock, but it had stitching and an elastic band.

Not the kind of thing a chicken would find lying around in the yard.

I gave it a sniff.

It smelled like baby powder.

"Where did you get this?" I asked.

"Get what?" said Dirt.

"The blindfold."

"Why, I reckon I don't know," said Sugar.

"We should skedaddle, ya hear?" said Dirt.

Neither of them had ever been farther south than the compost heap.

Dirt laughed so hard, she fell over.

That made the giggling stop.

So I knocked Sugar over, too.

"Where did you get the blindfold?" I repeated.

"I found it," answered Sugar from the floor.

"Where?" I asked.

"She doesn't remember," interrupted Dirt. "Besides, it's none of your—"

I moved the blindfold down to her mouth.

Silence at last.

The Scent of Worm

Moosh keeps a very close eye on all four of her chicks. Be a lot easier if she didn't have one eye on each side of her head.

But you gotta use the eyes you were dealt.

She ran in before my patience ran out.

And she brought Poppy and Sweetie with her.

I had Sugar under my paw, and Dirt was still tied to the rawhide.

Moosh didn't bat an eyelash.

"Time to go," she announced.

"Rabbit pee and dead worm," said Dirt.

"That's no way to talk to your mother," I said.

"In the *cups*," she added with a heavy sigh.

I took a sniff. She was right.

"How did you get rabbit pee?" I asked Sugar.

"There's only one way," she answered.

Nothing this kid does surprises me anymore.

"Tell me about the blindfold," I repeated.

"Lillian gave it to me," Sugar said.

"Who's Lillian?" I asked.

"My new friend," answered Sugar.

"The big white dog next door," explained Dirt. "Where have you been?"

I hadn't been next door since Bobby, the kid who lived there, had left for college about a month ago.

Bobby had a good arm and a ton of energy. I missed our daily games of fetch.

"What's Lillian's story?" I asked.

"She's beautiful," said Dirt.

"She calls me Little Boo," said Sugar.

"That's nauseating," I said.

"That happens to be my real name," she reminded me.

I hadn't used any of their real names since . . . well, since the first time I heard them and they annoyed me.

Moosh shot Sugar a look and led them all out.

She left the dead worm and the rabbit pee behind.

I got the better end of that deal.

The Price Is Right

Moosh is one smart chicken.

Even if Sugar didn't have the sense to know that *new friend* and *blindfold* should never show up in the same sentence, her mother should have.

It was clear that I needed more information.

It was also clear that I wasn't going to get it from anyone who didn't have lips.

There was only one place to go.

Vince the Funnel.

Vince was an inside dog with a mean streak and a plastic cone wrapped around his head. My water bowl spends more time outside than he does.

Vince and I weren't friends, but we had an understanding.

We understood that we didn't like each other.

I knocked on the doggie door at the back of the house.

It opened a sliver.

"Yeah," answered Vince.

His voice was thick and oozy—like a jelly doughnut on a hot dashboard.

"Lillian," I whispered.

"Never heard of her," he said.

He nudged the door open a tiny bit more with his nose.

I tossed in one of Barb's homemade dog biscuits.

"Diamond Lil," he said.

"Keep going," I said.

He cleared his throat.

"Name is Lillian—but they call her Diamond Lil on account of she's so shiny. Moved in about a week ago when the folks got lonely without the kid around. Word is she keeps to herself."

He stopped talking, but he didn't back away from the door.

"Anything else?" I asked.

"There might be . . ." he said.

He stuck his nose out of the doggie door.

"That was my last biscuit," I said.

The doggie door closed with a snap.

I heard his funnel scraping along the wall.

He was gone.

Old Dog, Old Tricks

*D*iamond Lil.

The words bounced around inside my brain.

It was beginning to give me a headache when Poppy and Sweetie came by.

They're a little odd to begin with, but they were even stranger than usual today. This morning was the first time the chickens had understayed their welcome.

I usually have to shove them out of my

doghouse to get a some peace.

Don't get me wrong—they're like family. Which is exactly why I can't spend all my time with them.

Poppy had a large rock on her head.

She stopped in front of me.

"Nice hat," I said.

"I'm working on my posture," she announced.

She began pacing back and forth.

"Since when do you care about your posture?" I asked.

"Good posture conveys power and confidence," said Sweetie.

"You should work on yours," added Poppy.

"Got all the confidence I need, thanks," I answered.

"I meant your posture," she said. "You're a little on the slouchy side."

"It makes you look old," said Poppy.

Hard to believe I was giving up sleep so these two sweethearts could insult me.

"While you're at it, your personality could use a little brushup, too," I said.

"Suit yourself, but it would really improve your image," Sweetie added.

I'm a search-and-rescue dog forced into retirement and walking the poultry beat in a country yard.

I didn't think I had an image.

I watched them practice their balancing

skills by walking along on top of the rocks that bordered the garden, then disappearing through a small hole at the bottom of the wooden fence.

It reminded me of my training days.

I couldn't have been much bigger than Poppy is now.

Actually, I was born bigger than Poppy is now, but you get the picture.

I spent hundreds of hours on the obstacle course, jumping over barrels, crawling through pipes and under boards, and balancing on ladders and shaky bridges.

All for a pat on the head and a liver treat for a job well done.

I got down low to look through the hole at the bottom of the fence.

I had been in that yard dozens of times tossing a stick with Bobby, but things look different when you're using one eye at ground level.

Then I saw her.

She was the shiniest mutt I'd ever laid eyes on.

Lillian was the size of a German shepherd, with a fluffy white coat and long full tail that curled along the ground, wrapping around her body.

She hopped up and gave Poppy and Sweetie each a big lick when she saw them coming through the fence.

I had licked Poppy exactly one time, when she fell into my food bowl.

The sound of tires on gravel grabbed my attention.

Someone was pulling into the driveway.

By the time the car door slammed a few seconds later, Lillian was out of sight and the chicks were on their way home.

I wasn't sure what Lillian had to do with baby powder and blindfolds, but I knew one thing for sure.

There's only one way a big, white, shiny mutt stays off my radar for a week.

On purpose.

Things That Go Bump in the Night

I started my patrol as usual that night, shortly after the sun went down.

After a quick head count, I circled around the chicken coop and then settled in around the front.

Anything that wanted to get in was going to have to go through me.

I closed my eyes and fell asleep.

A bright light hit me square in the face.

I jumped to my feet, ready for anything.

She was standing in front of me.

Lillian had set off the motion detector light in the yard, and her white coat was reflecting it—right into my face.

If I'd been a pile of dry sticks, she could have set me on fire.

"You're J.J.," she said.

"How about you tell me something I don't already know?" I grumbled.

"I'm Lillian," she said.

"Keep trying," I said.

She sat down in front of me, curling her long tail around her.

"Honey, where I was raised, when a new girl comes to town,

we give her a proper welcome. Maybe even a home-baked pie."

I was all out of pie.

"Where I come from, the only thing that comes knocking in the middle of the night is trouble," I said. "Not that you knocked."

"*Achoo!*"

It was a pretty tiny sneeze for a pretty big dog.

"*Achoo! Achoo!*"

Somebody inside the coop was sneezing.

"Join me for a walk?" said Lillian suddenly. "It's such a pretty night."

I didn't go in for moonlight strolls.

"Nights around here are for

rats and possums," I said.

"Honey, I'm no possum," she answered. "I'm a Samoyed—a purebred. I come from a long line of arctic guard dogs."

It wasn't a question, so I didn't answer it.

"Why don't you show me around?" she asked.

"Why don't you come back in the morning?" I answered.

"There's no starlight in the morning, darlin'." She seemed to be looking everywhere but up at the stars.

"Won't they be worried about you?" I asked.

"Who?" she answered.

She looked over her shoulder.

"Your owners," I said. "You know, Bobby's parents. . . ."

28

"Oh . . ." she said. "They fixed me up a beautiful bed in the kitchen. I just go out the doggie door whenever I please."

Barb's upstairs light flipped on.

I could see Vince's silhouette in the window.

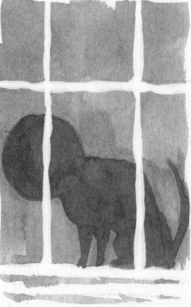

Lillian was done talking and I was done listening.

As she crossed the yard through the pool of light and then into the darkness, I couldn't help but notice—she did have really good posture.

Night Creatures

Moosh stuck her head through the door first thing in the morning. "I heard you had a visitor last night." I didn't have to look to know that she wasn't alone.

"Visitors bring cookies and small talk," I said. "She was more like an intruder."

"She's lovely. What are you talking about?" asked Moosh.

"She's fidgety," I said. "And she's wandering around in the middle of the night when she's got a perfectly warm dog bed inside. Doesn't make any sense."

"You're so suspicious," said Sugar.

"You could stand to be a little more suspicious yourself, Sugar," I said. "In case you've forgotten, the last time you made a new friend, you got us all kidnapped by Vince the Funnel."

"He has a point," said Dirt.

"Let it go," said Sugar.

"What are you doing over there, anyway?" I asked.

"Telling stories," answered Poppy.

Now I understood.

Lillian must have heard about some of my search-and-rescue adventures from the chicks. She must have been a little shy to come around during the day.

Poor kid was starstruck—I'd seen it before.

"If she wants to know anything about me," I chuckled, "she could have just asked."

"We're not telling her *your* stories, J.J.," said Moosh, cocking her head the way chickens do when they think you might have just embarrassed yourself.

"We're telling her *our* stories," said Poppy.

"You have stories?" I asked.

"Everyone has a story, J.J.," Moosh answered.

I wanted to say something else.

But I felt like a jerk.

I heard them leave.

They were short one set of feet.

"She's the new kid in town," said Sugar. "You should know how that feels."

I didn't turn around.

If you've never heard the sound of a tiny chicken's disappointed footsteps crunching through a thousand freshly fallen leaves scattered across a country yard while the light of the morning sun creeps its way across the sky—well, I hope you never do, pal.

The View from Down Under

Sitting alone in my doghouse with no one but myself for company wasn't nearly as much fun as I thought it was going to be.

Don't get me wrong, I'm an interesting guy—but I'd heard all my own stories.

I got to thinking about the first time I met Sugar. And how much she had annoyed me.

In fact, I hadn't liked any of them when I'd first met them.

I was wrong about Moosh and the chicks, so I guess there's a slight chance I could be wrong about the shiny new kid next door.

It was time for another conversation.

In daylight and on my terms.

I got a running start and scaled the fence in the yard.

Not bad—considering I was pushing seven.

I walked up to the old doghouse and cleared my throat.

"Lillian?"

No answer.

The doghouse was empty.

No Lillian.

No water bowl.

No squeaky toy.

It doesn't take a search-and-rescue dog to follow a trail of baby powder any more than it takes a firefighter to put out a match.

The scent got stronger as I got closer to the house—and led directly underneath it.

"I don't reckon you brought pie?" she said sweetly.

Again with the pie.

"What are you doing under there?" I asked.

"It's cooler under here," replied Lillian.

"Cool in the house too," I answered.

"I like fresh air," she said.

"Crawling under a house to get fresh air is a little like digging a hole to get some sun," I said.

"You sure got a funny way of apologizing, honey," she said.

"Listen, kid," I said. "I've got a family of chickens to protect, so I don't take kindly to anybody who arrives unannounced in the middle of the night. Won't apologize for that. If you and I are square . . ."

"Point taken," she said with a slight smile.

She wasn't looking for a fight.

"Say, how exactly does a fancy purebred arctic guard dog wind up in a country yard?" I asked.

"Same way a highly trained search-and-rescue dog does, I suppose," she said. "Besides," she added, "there's nothing fancy about me."

"You smell pretty fancy," I remarked.

"Aren't you sweet to notice!"

"I notice a lot," I said. "It's my job."

I was still crouching down under the house,

Halftime

I said yesterday, I was riding in the pickup truck," Moosh started. "Next new, we hit a bump and I landed about et off the side of the road. . . ."

to hand it to her, she was a great er.

had no problem imagining Barb run-into the middle of a soccer game to frightened chicken from the mouth of

and my legs were ready to give out.

"Listen, honey," she said softly, "seems like you and me got off on the wrong foot. How about you give a girl a second chance?"

"I suppose I—"

"Well, I do declare, look what the breeze blew in," Lillian interrupted. "I swear we got June bugs back home bigger than you, Little Boo."

Sugar's face lit up.

"We're about to have story time," said Dirt.

"Why don't you stay?" asked Moosh.

There was nothing much to do next door but chase squirrels.

Squirrels are pretty fast.

So I sat back down.

Sugar smiled.

"It's Mom's turn
going to finish the
Barb."

I never thought t
here.

I always figured

"Like
back of
thing I
twenty

I ha
storytel

I als
ning ou
rescue
a tuba.

My empty stomach let me know it was time to leave.

"How about some company on night patrol?" asked Lillian.

All the chickens were staring at me.

"It can be rough out there at night," I warned.

"I can handle it," she promised.

I hesitated, but Sugar gave me that look again.

I guess a little company wouldn't be the worst thing in the world, I thought.

"Okay," I said finally. "We'll give it a shot. But I don't want to hear blathering all night. It's a work shift, not a slumber party."

Sugar was ecstatic, Lillian looked pleased, and Moosh looked about as smug as a chicken can look without laying an egg.

Follow the Leader

Truth be told, I was looking forward to some canine company.

I missed my pals in search and rescue, even if we had only run into one another at training drills and natural disasters.

I had my doubts about Lillian, but then again, when you've seen as much of the world as I have, you tend to have doubts about almost everything.

I checked my distorted reflection in the

stainless steel water bowl.

My head looked huge.

And I had something in my teeth.

I heard her before I saw her.

"Howdy," she said.

She stepped out of the shadows but kept

far from the motion sensor.

She looked almost ghostly in the moonlight.

"Head count first," I told her.

We walked over to the chicken coop and peered in.

"Poppy sleeps in between Moosh and the wall," I said. "You just have to look really hard to find her."

"Who snores?" she giggled.

"That would be Sugar," I told her. "Can't stand to be quiet—even in her sleep. That kid is—"

"Achoo!"

A tiny sneeze came from the coop.

Lillian froze.

"I guess someone is catching a cold . . ." I said.

"*Click.*"

Lillian was looking past me toward the other side of our yard, opposite her own.

Another sneeze.

"*Click.*"

Lillian's back went rigid, her tail stood up straight, and her eyes were wide.

She took off like a shot and pounced at the bottom of the fence.

"Come on!" she yelled over her shoulder. "Something came over the fence!"

It was hard to keep up with her.

Lillian kept moving farther along the fence—almost to the back corner of the property. I couldn't even see the chicken coop from back there.

I didn't know what I was trying to track, so none of the smells along the fence were any help.

I was steps away from the farthest corner of the yard when I heard a scream I will never forget.

I'd heard Moosh nag, cry, laugh, yell, whine, and cluck—I'd even heard her sing "The Star-Spangled Banner" once—but I'd never heard her scream.

I was airborne.

One split second later, I got an eyeful of dirt from Lillian's back paws as she ran past me.

She leaped over two lawn chairs, shimmied under the picnic bench, and shot like a rocket through the old tire swing.

The force of Lillian's body hit the chicken coop like a cannonball.

Moosh was shaking, and all the color had drained from her face.

"What happened?" I panted.

She was in shock.

"Take it easy," I said. "Tell me what happened."

Lillian wrapped her up in her tail.

"I heard a thud on the roof," Moosh began slowly.

The color was coming back to her beak.

"I called for you . . ." she said, looking at me with one hard, unforgiving eye.

"You left us alone," she said.

She turned her head. The other eye was just as mad.

"She was right here," she said.

"Who was?" asked Lillian. "Who was here?"

"The possum," Moosh answered.

I looked at Lillian and she looked at me.

"What did she say?" asked Lillian.

I may not know much about possums, but I was pretty sure they weren't known for making conversation.

"She didn't *say* anything," said Moosh. "She must have heard you coming. She took off."

Moosh turned to me again. "Where were you?" she demanded.

"I was in the corner of the yard," I began. "I was . . ."

"It's okay," said Lillian. "Everything is okay now, Mama."

Moosh took her angry eyes back into the chicken coop.

Lillian and I took up positions in front of the door.

"Maybe the possum didn't mean any harm," said Lillian. "She had her chance to grab Moosh . . . and she didn't."

I looked at her a good long time.

I wasn't just protecting the chickens for the chickens' sake. I was protecting them for Barb. We'd been through thick and thin together, saved lives together, saved each other even.

"Listen to me, kid," I said. "That possum so much as breathes the same air as these chickens and it's a goner."

She hung her head.

"I told you it might get rough out here," I said.

"And I told you I could handle it," insisted Lillian.

I hoped she was right.

11

Ghost Trails

I didn't get a wink of sleep that night.

It was lucky for all of us that Lillian was here. She had beaten me back to the chicken coop by at least three seconds.

May not sound like a lot, but three seconds in a showdown between a chicken and a possum is enough to decide which one of them will still be there when you get to four.

Lillian could have meant the difference

between Moosh surviving and—well, the alternative.

Lillian went back to her yard when the sun came up.

I tried to talk her into getting some sleep, but she wouldn't have it.

After she left, I decided to do some scent work.

I walked to the first gray post at the back of the property, my tail running along the rough wood. The fence was old and weathered and had probably been around since before the house was built. I stopped and looked behind me every couple of feet to see if anyone or anything was watching.

For such an old fence, it was in pretty good shape. No loose boards, no holes—at least nothing a possum could use.

I made my way all the way to the front of the property.

I didn't pick up a possum scent.

But I had a good idea where the rabbits were peeing.

I was missing scents, leaving the chickens vulnerable, and as tired as I had ever been.

Keeping the chickens safe was a job I wasn't going to be able to do on my own.

I needed a partner.

Someone quick.

Someone smart.

Someone I could trust.

Someone like Lillian.

Once upon a Time . . .

"What you need is a little dab of cornstarch." Lillian was entertaining the chickens under Bobby's house again.

She was doing a great job distracting Moosh from the events of the night before.

Luckily, chickens play hard and sleep hard.

None of the chicks knew about Moosh's close call with a possum.

Lillian looked up and gave me a wink.

"Cornstarch?" asked Sweetie. "For real?"

"You bet your bacon, honey," said Lillian. "A little cornstarch or some baby powder fluffs up white fur and makes it look nice and bright."

"Would it work on feathers?" asked Sugar.

"It might, Little Boo," she replied. "Trick is you have to brush it out."

"Or what?" I asked.

"Or . . ." Lillian said with a smile, "your nose begins to twitch a little bit, and right when the judge comes over, you sneeze in her face and cover her with a dust cloud of white powder!"

"You did *not!*" said Dirt, laughing.

"Sure did, honey," chuckled Lillian. "Ruined her Sunday best while I was at it!"

"Your owner was a judge?" asked Moosh with a cocked head.

"I near 'bout blew the curl right out of her hair," said Lillian.

Even Moosh had to laugh.

"Your turn," said Lillian.

"For what?" I answered.

"A story," she said.

"I do have some good ones . . ." I began.

"Not the flash flood one," said Sugar.

"Or the avalanche one," groaned Dirt.

"Anything but the ski rescue that you tell with a French accent," added Sweetie.

"Perhaps the thrilling story about the time you ran screaming from a butterfly," I growled.

"She was chasing me!" cried Sweetie.

Just then, Barb called the chickens for lunch.

I walked them to the fence and waited till

they had gone through the hole.

I got down and took a peek as Barb spread the chicken feed outside the coop.

Something had been bothering me, and it was time to get it out.

"What's with the blindfold?" I asked.

"It's a sleep mask, actually," Lillian answered quickly. "I don't use it much anymore, and Sugar seemed to really like it."

I nodded.

"How did you know it was mine?" she asked.

"You both smell like baby powder," I replied.

She nodded.

"That, plus Sugar told me," I admitted.

"I've love to hear a rescue story," Lillian said suddenly.

"Maybe another time," I said. "I've got to

catch up on my sleep."

"Tell me about the flash flood," she pleaded.

I shook my head.

"Pretty please . . ." she said.

I had to admit—it was a good one.

"Okay. I was hot on the trail of a middle-aged man last seen minutes before a flash flood struck his camp-site. The scent was heavy, but the following was hard . . . so much debris and the water was still rising. . . ."

Lillian was hanging on my every word.

"There were helicopters overhead, park

rangers barking on bullhorns; and the ground was teeming with snakes and TV reporters. I could barely walk from here to there without stepping on one," I said.

"You stepped on a snake?" gasped Lillian.

"No," I said, "a TV reporter."

"Flash floods are about as predictable as a crazy dream after one too many fish tacos—one minute you're fine, and the next minute a moose is floating past you wearing a fishing hat and ladies' pajamas."

Lillian was mesmerized.

"I was in water up to my neck when I heard the first crack of thunder. It was about that time I got the first whiff of gas. I couldn't see the bottom of the debris pile, but my guess was a propane tank—a big one. I barked like crazy

to let Barb know that we had to hightail it out of there . . ."

I paused for dramatic effect.

Lillian hadn't moved a muscle.

"I jumped on Barb to give her a head start on a stop, drop, and roll. We hit the ground tumbling. Sure enough, lightning struck and blew up the tank. The debris was on fire, and Barb lost three inches of her ponytail in a puff of smoke. . . ."

Lillian was shaking her head in disbelief.

"We didn't stop rolling until we hit the bottom of a tree twelve feet away. I'm lying on my back with the smell of burned hair in my nose, and that's when . . . I look up the tree and see my lost camper clinging to a branch twenty feet up."

"Do go on!"

"Poor guy was in shock— couldn't even yell for help."

"Well, shut my mouth," Lillian said. "Up in a tree. . . ."

"Yep," I said. "Sometimes you have to get your nose out of the ground to find what you're looking for."

Up, Up, and Away

Soon after the chickens were fed, it was my turn to head home and eat.

They were waiting for me in front of my food bowl.

"You two certainly seem to be getting along," said Moosh.

"You didn't bore her with one of your stories, did you?" asked Sugar.

"Not the flash flood one," said Dirt.

"Or the avalanche one," groaned Poppy.

"Please tell me you didn't embarrass yourself with a French accent," added Sweetie.

"As a matter of fact, I told her about the flash flood rescue," I said. "And she was riveted."

"That was a great story," said Sugar, "the first eight times I heard it."

"Yeah," said Sweetie. "What kind of search-and-rescue dog forgets to look up?"

Sweetie was too big to ignore and too light to be a paperweight, but she had finally made herself useful.

The whole time I had been tracking—and losing—that possum, I had never looked up.

I scaled the wall of the chicken coop the same way I had scaled the fence.

I wasn't up there for more than two heart-beats when I heard it.

Thud!

I turned around with my teeth bared, expecting to come face-to-face with a possum.

Instead, I was face-to-face with Moosh.

"I'm sorry about the other night," she said. "I shouldn't have snapped at you like that."

"Not half as sorry as I am," I answered.

"What did you see back there?" she asked.

"I didn't actually see anything," I said. "Lillian did."

"What did she see?" asked Moosh.

"I'm not sure," I said.

"Did you pick up a trail, at least?" she asked.

"Nope," I said. "Nothing."

"Funny," she said.

I hadn't picked up a scent I could use along the fence, but I was definitely picking up one on the roof.

There was nothing funny about that.

The oak tree was at least twenty feet away, but one of its branches reached almost to the top of the coop.

It took less than a minute on the roof to see how the possum was getting into the yard.

I could also see into Bobby's family's kitchen window.

Bobby's dad was filling a teakettle with water from the sink. He put the kettle down and turned on the stove. He switched on a radio, then stopped in front of Bobby's pictures

on the fridge and smiled.

Then he set out a teacup and cut himself a nice big slice of pie.

It sure looked like Lillian had found herself the perfect home.

Night Shift Part Two

The sun was getting low in the sky.

I decided to head over to Lillian's before she headed over to me.

"Honey," she said, "you look like the back side of bad weather."

"That doesn't sound like a compliment."

"It isn't." She laughed. "You oughtta go to sleep with the chickens tonight."

"The chicken coop is not really built for a guy like me," I said.

"Back home, that means get to bed early," she explained. "Let me take the night shift tonight. You know I can handle it."

"That *was* some fancy footwork last night," I said. "If I didn't know any better, I'd say you'd had some kind of training."

"Oh, honey, I've been chasing night critters

since I was knee-high to a grasshopper," she answered.

"Do you ever get homesick?" I asked.

"I do miss sitting on the front porch," she said.

"And the pie," I said, laughing. "Don't forget the pie."

"Seems like the only way to get some people to hush is to bring pie. That way they're too busy chewing to interrupt the storytelling!" she said.

"Where did you say home was, again?" I asked.

"Why, I'm not sure I ever did," she said. "I was born and raised in Georgia."

"That's a long way from here," I said.

"It sure is, honey," she said. "I was with Ida

Rose for six years. She was an old-fashioned Southern belle, just as lovely as lovely can get. But as she got on in years, I'm afraid I was just too much dog for her."

I waited for her to continue.

"She moved in with her daughter—who was happy to have her mama, but not so happy to have her mama's big old dog." She smiled. "And now I'm here."

"I guess they got a little lonely next door when Bobby left for college," I suggested.

"Lucky for me," she said.

"Bobby will be home soon for Thanksgiving," I said. "You'll be playing fetch all day long."

"Heaven knows they talk about him all the time," she said. "I can't wait to meet that handsome boy in person."

Bobby was a good kid with a great arm—but *handsome* wasn't a word I would use.

Bobby was short for *Roberta*.

Let the Sun Shine

"**Y**ou feeling okay?" I asked.

"Fit as a fiddle, darlin'," Lillian said. "Why?"

"You just said handsome 'boy,'" I said, "but Bobby's a girl."

"Did I really?" she answered. "Of course she's a girl! Silly me."

"Hmm," I said. "Maybe you're the one who needs to catch up on some sleep."

I gave her a nod and crawled out from under the house.

On the short walk back home I considered what I knew about Lillian.

Could be sleep deprivation. I once stayed up two days straight on an SAR job and forgot my own name.

She didn't know that Bobby was a girl—and although she hadn't met her, I knew for a fact that there were pictures of her plastered all over the refrigerator.

Lillian also spent most of the day under the house.

Come to think of it, I'd never had a conversation with her out in the light of day.

She'd also never told me what she had seen in the yard that night—because maybe she didn't really know.

Maybe her owner wasn't the one who was

getting on in years and feeling poorly—maybe it was the other way around.

It got me thinking of a search-and-rescue dog out of Topeka named Dutch.

Old Dutch developed some kind of problem with his eyes—and sunlight only made it worse.

He had a crazy-looking pair of sunglasses he would wear when he had to be out in the daytime.

He looked like kind of ridiculous, but Dutch was not a mutt you wanted to mess with.

Besides, as far as search and rescue goes, you could wear a tutu and an Easter bonnet as long as you come back with what you went out looking to find.

There was no way to reach out to Dutch—I

needed somebody closer to home.

Lucky for me, I had a pretty good idea of where I might find a dog with some medical issues.

I Hear You Knocking

I knocked on the doggie door at the back of the house.

It opened a sliver.

"Yeah?" answered Vince.

His voice was thin and sharp—like something really thin and sharp.

"Sunglasses," I said.

The doggie door opened just enough for a biscuit.

I didn't have a biscuit.

I pushed the whole front half of my body through the door

Then I stuck my face inside his ridiculous funnel.

"You wore them for a while," I said. "Why?"

"Complications from an eye infection," he said.

"Go get them," I growled.

Vince ran upstairs on his stumpy legs.

LOST!

While he was gone, I made myself comfortable in the kitchen.

The refrigerator was plastered with pictures of me and Barb.

There we are at the tracking and avalanche seminar in Colorado.

And there we are with a bunch of the guys when we flew down to Haiti after the earthquake.

A notice for a lost dog.

It was on top of a newspaper clipping of one of our last gigs together—a building collapse in downtown Philadelphia.

That was a good rescue. I'd have to remember to tell Lillian about it.

A listing of pets from the animal shelter that needed new homes.

Mr. Smoochy, a gray kitten, was at the top of the list.

Even a chick the size of an empanada could give a cat named Mr. Smoochy a hard time. Poor kid was gonna need a new name no matter where he went.

I heard the funnel scraping along the wall as Vince came down the stairs.

He handed me a pair of doggie sunglasses. "Why does Hero Dog need a pair of sunglasses?" asked Vince. "In case you hadn't noticed, your days of photographers and newspaper clippings are over."

"If I thought I owed you an explanation, I would have given it to you already," I said.

Vince used his tongue to suck something out of his teeth.

"I'm not sure they're gonna fit your new *friend*," he said.

"When her business is your business, you'll be the first to know," I said as I turned away.

"I didn't think you'd sink any lower, J.J.," he said. "From hometown hero to chicken body-guard—and now errand boy."

"If you were any less of a dog, you'd need a litter box," I said.

"Chump," he muttered.

"You looking to start something here, Vince?" I asked.

"Lillian's not telling you everything," said Vince.

I put my face inside his funnel again.

"You don't know anything about her," I said.

"If you say so," he said with a half smile.

I wanted to stare him down, but the double dose of dog breath in the funnel was getting to me.

I picked up the glasses in my mouth and headed toward the doggie door.

I turned around to face him one last time.

"You got anything else to say?" I asked.

"Not yet," he answered.

Slumber Party

Lillian entered the yard shortly after midnight, just as we had agreed.

She stuck to the shadows as usual and looked around the yard.

"Hey," I said.

"Hey back," she replied, smiling.

"Just did a head count," I said. "Everyone is exactly where they should be."

"You go on and get some rest," she said. "I'll wake you up if I need you."

"Thanks, partner," I said.

I headed back to my doghouse.

I had decided to take her advice to go to sleep with the chickens, but not in the way she meant it.

Moosh and the chicks were waiting for me inside.

"I still don't understand what we're doing here," said Moosh.

"It's safer than the chicken coop," I said.

Truth is, I was worried about Lillian's eyesight and wasn't sure she could handle the shift on her own.

I might have been a little rough on the kid the night before, and she wanted the chance to prove herself.

This way she could do it without anyone getting hurt.

I didn't want to hurt Lillian's feelings or embarrass her, so I had Moosh and the chicks in the doghouse with me.

I put the sunglasses around my neck for safekeeping.

I would give them to Lillian tomorrow when

nobody was around.

I gave up my dog bed to the chicks, and they were warm and comfortable despite the open door and the cool night.

Moosh headed back to settle in with the chicks, who were all sound asleep.

I laid my body down right inside the door and wrapped my tail around so that it just covered my eyes.

The sounds of the night were standard issue.

An occasional passing car.

Windows opening and closing.

The hoot of an unseen owl.

Then—there it was.

An unmistakable . . . *thud!*

Lillian heard it too.

She turned her head and then stood up.

Her posture and tail were relaxed and casual—not standing straight up in alarm like the night before.

It was clear she wasn't looking for a possum. She was waiting for it.

Strange Company

The possum came out of the shadows, confident and comfortable, despite the lurking figure of a fifty-pound dog.

Lillian looked around the yard and then stepped aside.

"Make it quick, Ida," said Lillian. "And keep it quiet, will ya? Those chicks will sleep through just about anything, but Moosh is another story."

There wasn't a hint of Georgia in her accent.

The possum walked into the chicken coop like she owned it.

Moosh had come up behind me and saw the same thing I did.

She was trying to force her way past me.

I muzzled her with my tail and kept her still.

I could hear rustling and hissing from inside the chicken coop.

Moosh's eyes got as wide as I'd ever seen.

The possum was tearing that place apart.

I couldn't stand it anymore.

Neither could Moosh.

She ran over me, across the yard, and headed right toward Lillian.

I caught up with her and got in between them.

"Run, Ida!" Lillian yelled.

Ida came racing out of the coop and ran right past me.

I didn't know Sugar was in the yard until I saw Ida swoop her up in her paws.

"*Let her go!*" I barked.

"Not a chance," Ida answered.

Lillian went nose-to-nose with Ida.

"This wasn't our deal, Ida," she said. "Put the chick down."

Sugar was now dangling from Ida's mouth, pale and breathing fast.

If I pounced, Sugar was a goner.

Lillian turned to me.

"Listen, J.J.," said Lillian. "Just do what I say, and everything will be fine."

"I've wasted enough time listening to you," I said.

Right then and there it hit me like a ton of bricks.

Since the first night I'd met her, she'd been trying to get me away from the chicken coop.

There was the invitation for a midnight stroll and the wild-goose chase to the back fence, and tonight she had convinced me to let her handle the night patrol alone.

I finally realized that Lillian had never set paw in Bobby's house.

She wasn't living next door—she was hiding there.

I had been so busy tracking the shadow of a possum that I'd missed what was standing right in front of me.

A big, white, shiny lie.

Lillian didn't have a problem with her eyes.

She had a problem with the truth.

Mama to Mama

"**I**'m just trying to help out my friend here, so you're gonna back off, you're gonna do what I say, and you're gonna let Ida Rose get what she came here for."

Ida Rose . . . at least the name was real. We were at a standstill.

"Everything is going to be okay, Little Boo," said Moosh. "Mama's here."

She was walking slowly toward Ida.

Ida took Sugar out of her mouth and held

her in her claws.

"I'm not leaving until I get what I want," said Ida.

Moosh was within an inch of Ida's face now.

"That's my baby you have in your paws," said Moosh.

Ida was having a hard time looking Moosh in the eye.

"I know what you really want," said Moosh.

"Moosh," I said. "Don't do it."

She ignored me.

"You're going to put Sugar down now. And you and I are going into the chicken coop."

I made a move toward them, but Ida grabbed Sugar even tighter and Moosh waved me off.

"I'll handle this, J.J.," said Moosh. "Ida Rose is going to put Sugar down now . . . and you're going to let her pass."

"I don't know about this, Ida," said Lillian.

"You've done enough damage," spat Moosh.

I never thought I'd see a grown dog back down from an aging chicken—but this night was full of firsts.

Lillian did what she was told.

Ida let go of Sugar without ever taking her eyes off Moosh.

I picked Sugar up with my teeth and held her there like a newborn pup.

She was still shaking.

"Me and Ida here are going into the chicken coop," said Moosh. "And we're going in alone."

The Longest Minute

The rest of the chicks had finally made their way out of the doghouse.

I could tell by their faces that they had seen enough to be terrified.

Inside the coop, there was silence.

If anything happened to Moosh, Lillian was going to answer for it.

I was so tense, I didn't think I could move if I wanted to.

Moosh was one tough chicken, but I didn't

know if she could survive a throwdown with a possum.

I needed to hear something—anything—that would let me know what was going on in there—and give me a chance to do something about it.

A minute went by . . . and still nothing.

Finally the first tiny sounds slipped out of the chicken coop.

"Achoo."

"Click."

"Achoo."

"Click."

"Achoo."

"Click."

Seconds later, I saw the single strangest thing I have ever seen—and I once saw a moose float past me in ladies' pajamas.

I saw a chicken and a possum walk out of the coop side by side.

"*Achoo.*"

The tiny head of a young possum was sticking out of Ida's pouch.

"*Click.*"

Old News

"Ida Rose got separated from her little girl a few days ago," explained Lillian with tears in her eyes.

"How did you know she was in the coop?" I asked.

"A baby possum sneezes to call for its mother," Ida Rose answered. "And the mother clicks to answer it. We had both heard it, but I couldn't risk going in with you protecting the chickens."

Ida turned to Moosh.

"Thank you for keeping her warm every night," she said.

There was plenty of hay and plenty of food on the floor in the chicken coop. Moosh had actually been keeping the little thing warm every night the same way she kept her eggs warm—by sitting on top of her.

The only difference was, Moosh had no idea she was there.

"How did you know Ida wasn't going to hurt you?" I asked Moosh.

"There's only one reason a possum would keep coming back to this yard with a dog hot on its trail—to protect her own," she said.

I had Lillian's sunglasses around my neck and I felt like a fool.

I wasn't even sure where to begin.

"You're not from Georgia, are you?" I asked, even though I knew the answer.

Lillian shook her head.

She was having a hard time looking any of us in the eye.

"How did you wind up keeping company with a possum?" I asked Lillian.

"I met Ida Rose under the house next door," she explained. "I'd been hiding there."

"We were both scared and alone," said Ida. "I took a chance and asked a dog for help—and got it."

"Why didn't you just ask *me* for help?" I asked.

"Ask you to help a possum?"

The upstairs light flipped on.

"So who are you?" I asked.

"Nobody," Lillian said sadly. "I'm nobody. I'll be going now. I never meant to cause any trouble."

"She's a fugitive," said a voice from the shadows.

We all turned to see Vince walking toward us.

He was carrying something in his mouth.

He tripped over the garden hose and landed facedown in front of the coop.

The funnel was stuck in the loose ground, and his legs and tail were flailing out of the top end.

His muffled voice came out from under the funnel.

"She's a show dog," said Vince. "A fugitive show dog." He placed his paw on the paper he'd dropped when he fell.

Moosh has a much bigger heart than I do, and she pushed him over so he could get back on his feet.

"You'll be captured any minute now, *Diamond Lil,*" cackled Vince. "And that's all that matters."

LOST!

REWARD REWARD REWARD
Lillian
Last Seen September 12th outside our home in Princeton, New Jersey.

Lillian is a six-year-old Samoyed and a champion show dog. We miss her terribly.

Please call Alix at 555-111-6776 or email LostLillian@yahoo.com.

The picture left no doubt.

There was Lillian with a big smile on her face and a blue ribbon around her neck.

There's No Place Like Home

"The agility jumps, the beauty tips, the posture," I said, "it all makes sense. You really are a champion show dog."

"No," said Lillian, shaking her head.

"Lillian, that's you in the picture," I said. "It's time to stop lying."

"Yes, it's me," she said. "But I'm no champion."

"It's you or it isn't," I said gruffly.

"That's not what I meant," she said. "I

meant I'm not actually *lost*."

"Nice try, Beauty Queen," said Vince.

"I ran away," she said.

"Why?" I asked.

"I'm not a champion anymore. I stopped winning. I was hoping they didn't really care so much about the ribbons and the trophies, but I heard Alix on the phone one day trying to get rid of me."

"That's terrible," said Moosh.

"I left that day, and I've been on my own ever since. Ida Rose was the first friend I'd made in a long time . . . and then I met you all."

Moosh was shaking her head.

"I understand," Lillian said. "I'm sorry I made all that stuff up. I don't deserve to be your friend."

"Why would they be looking for you if they didn't want you?"

"To sell me, I guess," she said. "Champions—even former champions—can go for a lot of money."

Barb had heard all the commotion and was standing at the back door.

"What's going to happen now?" asked Sugar.

"I'm going to stop running," said Lillian.

She picked up the LOST notice in her teeth and walked across the yard, directly under the bright light, and right through the kitchen door.

She was turning herself in.

There wasn't a dry eye in the yard.

Except mine.

Search-and-rescue dogs don't cry.

But we occasionally get debris in our eyes
and then they water up a bit.

Good thing I had those sunglasses.

Epilogue

Barb did exactly what we knew she would do—she gave Lillian a good meal and a warm bed and then called the number on the LOST flyer. It was true Lillian hadn't won any ribbons lately, but Alix, her owner, didn't care about that. She had been looking to find Lillian a new home because she was moving overseas to join the Peace Corps. She was just thrilled to know that Lillian was okay and insisted that Barb take the reward money. Barb, being

Barb, donated it to the local animal shelter.

After a long talk with Bobby's dad, Barb knew that Lillian had found the home she was meant to have. The family fixed up the dog-house and got her a great big fancy dog bed for the kitchen—and, of course, a doggie door. I gave her the doggie sunglasses as a welcome present—she wears them all the time. She doesn't need them, really, but she says it's rude to turn down a gift.

Search-and-rescue dog J.J. Tully is about to meet his match...

A National Indie Bestseller

DOREEN CRONIN is the *New York Times* bestselling author of favorite picture books such as *Rescue Bunnies*, the Diary of . . . series, and *Click, Clack, Moo: Cows That Type*, a Caldecott Honor Book. She also wrote *The Trouble with Chickens*, the first book in the J.J. Tully Mystery series. When she was growing up, Doreen's dogs were Archie and Trapper (after two of her favorite television characters). She lives in Brooklyn, New York. You can visit her online at www.doreencronin.com.

KEVIN CORNELL spends his days writing and drawing from his doghouse outside Philadelphia, Pennsylvania. He can do several popular tricks, including "Sit," "Stay," and "Illustrate Books"— such as *The Trouble with Chickens*, *The Curious Case of Benjamin Button: A Graphic Novel*, and *Mustache!* by Mac Barnett. Visit him online at www.kevskinrug.com.